# The Nicest Naughtiest Fairy

written and
illustrated by

## Nick Ward

Albury Children's

For Jade,
Who thought I had
forgotten her! N.W.

First published in 2004 by Meadowside Children's Books,

This edition published in 2014 by Albury Books, Albury Court, Albury, Thame,

OX9 2LP, United Kingdom

For orders: Kuperard Publishers and Distributors +44 (0) 2084462440

Text © Nick Ward · Illustrations © Nick Ward

The rights of Nick Ward to be identified as the author and illustrator have been

asserted by them in accordance with the Copyright, Designs and Patents Act, 1988

ISBN 978-1-909958-34-0 (paperback)

A CIP catalogue record for this book is available from the British Library

Printed in China

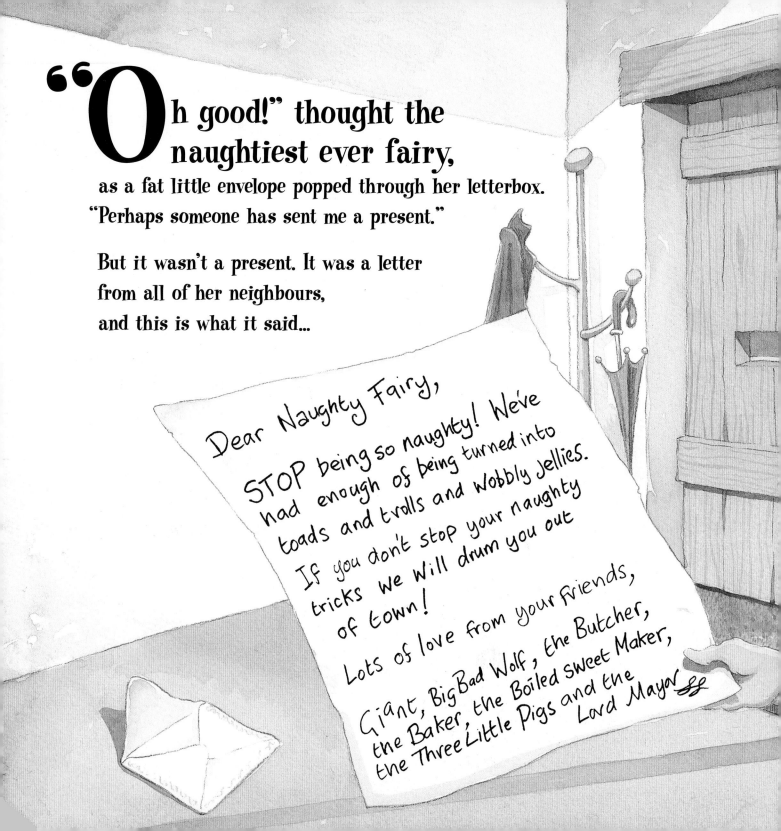

"**O**h good!" thought the naughtiest ever fairy, as a fat little envelope popped through her letterbox. "Perhaps someone has sent me a present."

But it wasn't a present. It was a letter from all of her neighbours, and this is what it said...

Dear Naughty Fairy,

STOP being so naughty! We've had enough of being turned into toads and trolls and wobbly jellies. If you don't stop your naughty tricks we will drum you out of town!

Lots of love from your friends,

Giant, Big Bad Wolf, the Butcher, the Baker, the Boiled Sweet Maker, the Three Little Pigs and the Lord Mayor

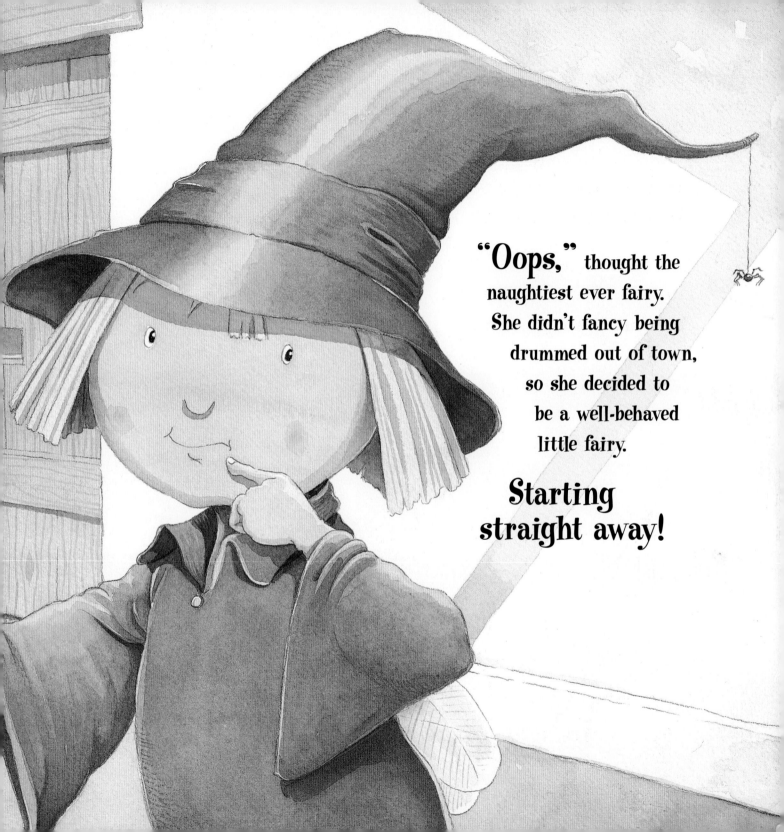

**"Oops,"** thought the naughtiest ever fairy. She didn't fancy being drummed out of town, so she decided to be a well-behaved little fairy.

**Starting straight away!**

The very noisy giant was busy
crashing about, spring-cleaning
his castle when the well-behaved
naughty fairy arrived.

"I can help you with that,"
she shouted above the din.

GRANNY GIANT.

"No!" cried the noisy giant.
"I know your naughty tricks."
"Don't worry, I'm a well-behaved naughty
fairy." She smiled sweetly
and waved her
magic wand.

But although
the naughty
fairy tried to be
good, her magic
was determined to
be especially naughty,
and almost at once things
started to go wrong...

The vacuum sucked up the rubbish,
the rugs and just about everything else!

Soon it was so full,
it exploded in a cloud of dust.

**"Sorry,"**
said the good naughty fairy
and quickly flew off to help
somebody else.

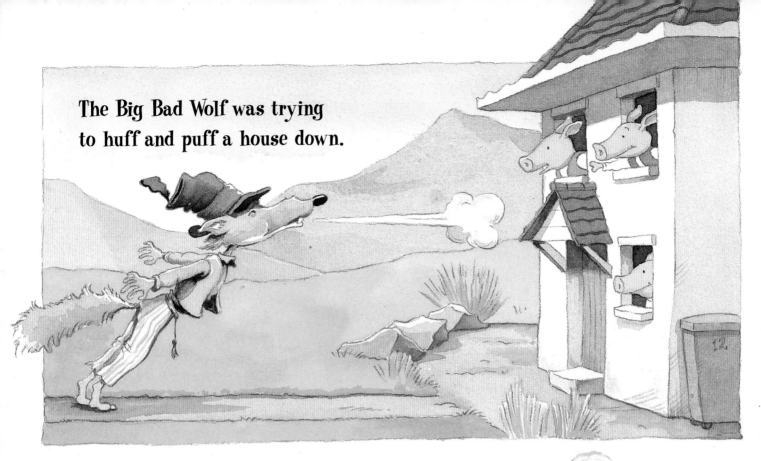

The Big Bad Wolf was trying to huff and puff a house down.

**"Oh, please let me help,"** volunteered the good naughty fairy, and summoned up a wind so strong it blew the wolf's clothes right off and sent the house spinning across the valley and far out to sea...

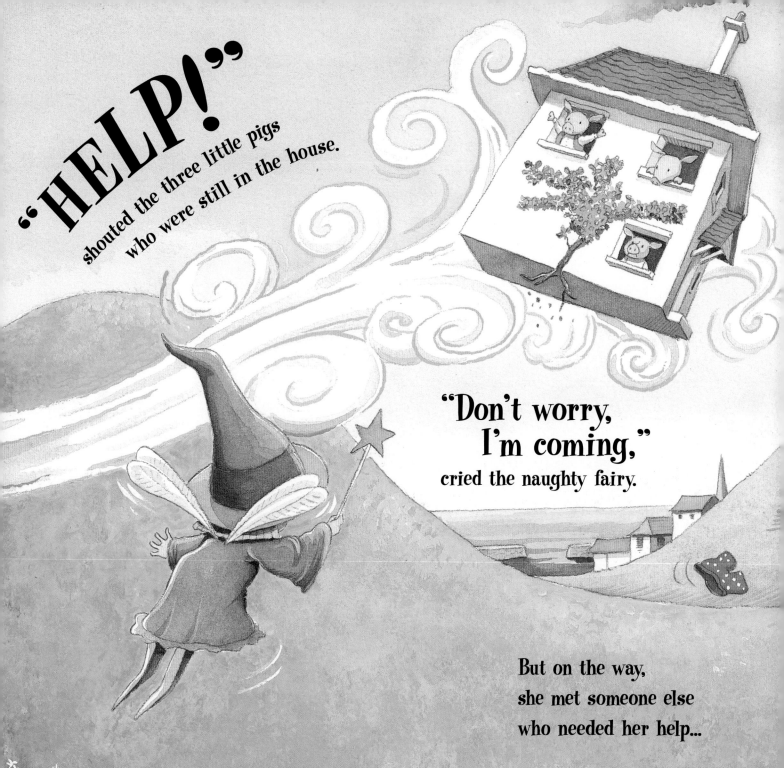

"**HELP!**" shouted the three little pigs who were still in the house.

"**Don't worry, I'm coming,**" cried the naughty fairy.

But on the way, she met someone else who needed her help...

The boiled
sweet maker
lived at the top of
a steep hill and he was
mixing a huge pot of sweet
smelling candy, when the
naughty fairy passed by.

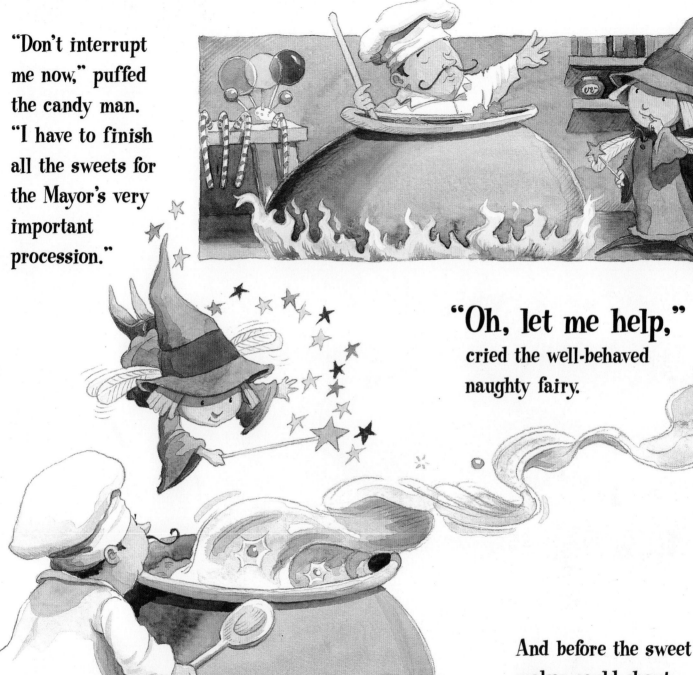

"Don't interrupt me now," puffed the candy man. "I have to finish all the sweets for the Mayor's very important procession."

**"Oh, let me help,"** cried the well-behaved naughty fairy.

And before the sweet maker could shout **"No!"** she had waved her magic wand.

KAZAM!

The pot began to rattle and shake, and **WOOSH!** the gooey mixture erupted out of the pot, spilling across the floor. **"Stop it!"** cried the sweet maker as the sticky mess bubbled out of the door and down the hill. But the well-behaved naughty fairy had already gone.

All the way down the hill townsfolk were getting
stuck in the mucky mess. The Mayor's important
procession had been bought to a standstill,
up to their knees in toffee.

"I might have known
it was you," yelled the
Mayor, shaking his fist as
the naughty fairy flew by.

Soon the naughty fairy came upon the bold and roaring lion (who was king of the jungle). He was having a royal nap. "Ah, he's sleeping like a baby, said the helpful fairy. "I'll just make him a little more comfortable." She waved her magic wand and...

**KAZAM!**

The mighty king of the jungle awoke to find himself dressed in a baby's bonnet and nappy, rocking in a cradle!

"How embarrassing," he roared.

"Just you wait!"

Big Bab

But by now the naughty fairy had flown out
to sea to help the three little pigs,
whose house was still bobbing
about on the waves.
**"Fairy to the rescue!"**
she cried, waving her
magic wand...

KAZAM!

A huge and
hungry whale
arched out of the
sea and gobbled up the
pigs and their house
in one mouthful!

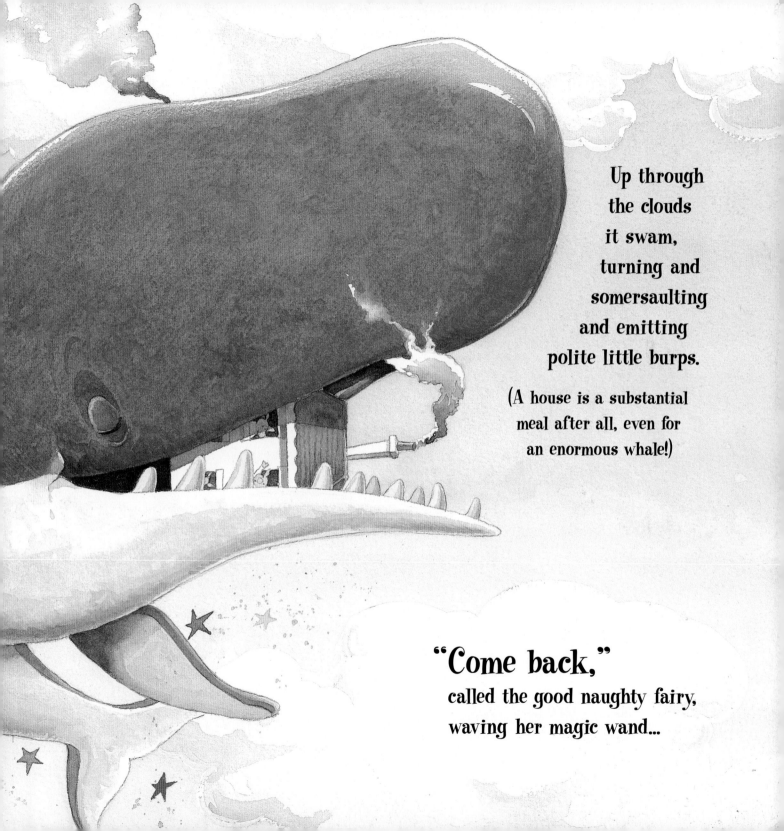

Up through
the clouds
it swam,
turning and
somersaulting
and emitting
polite little burps.

(A house is a substantial
meal after all, even for
an enormous whale!)

**"Come back,"**
called the good naughty fairy,
waving her magic wand...

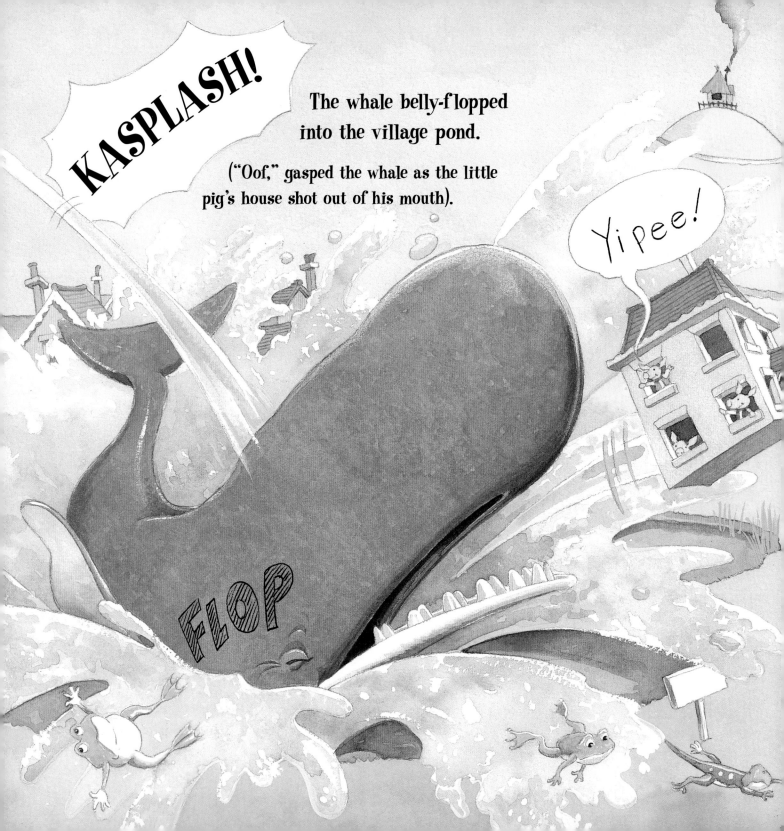

Pond water and pond life rained down on the town. Mrs Munchet, the schoolteacher, was covered in slime and weeds and frogspawn...

**KASPLOSH!**

The baker's magnificent cake for the Mayor's procession was drenched in pond water...

And the last of the fiery dragon's fiery breath was snuffed out in the downpour.

**"This is one of the naughty fairy's tricks,"** they spluttered.

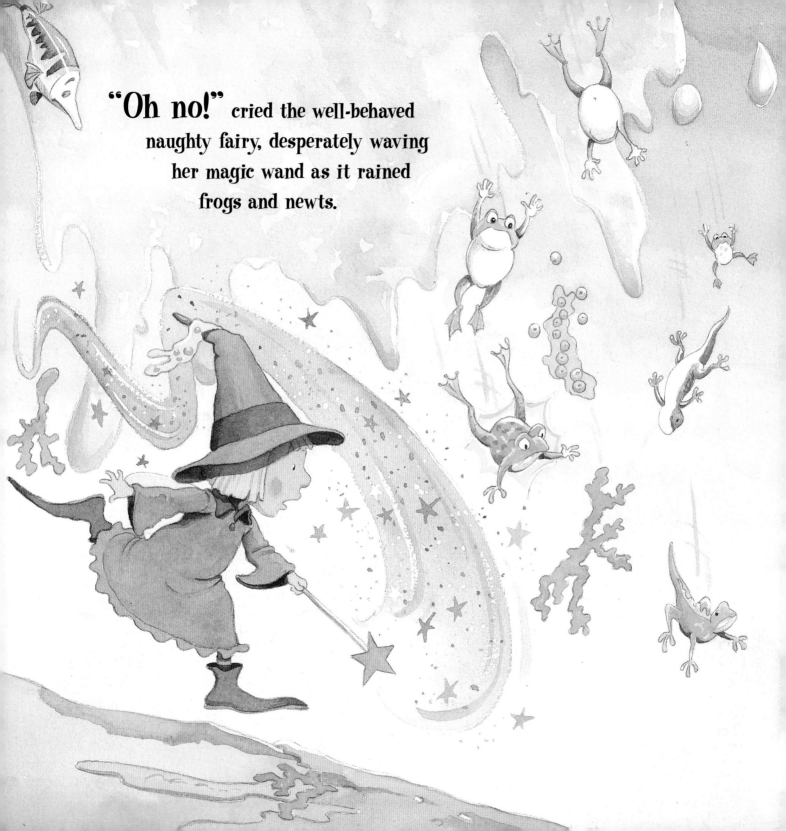

"Oh no!" cried the well-behaved naughty fairy, desperately waving her magic wand as it rained frogs and newts.

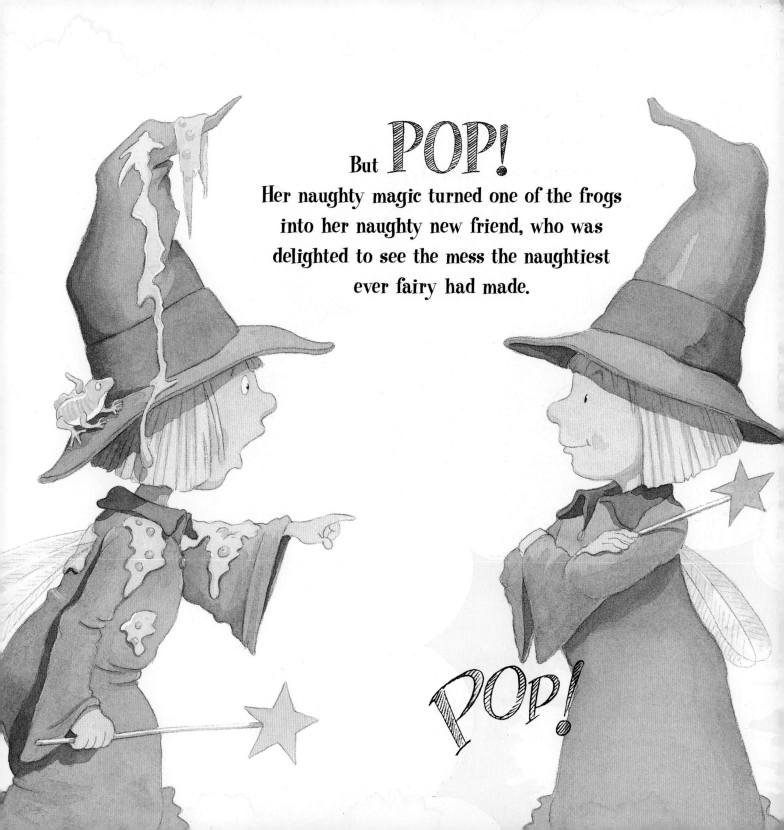

But **POP!**
Her naughty magic turned one of the frogs
into her naughty new friend, who was
delighted to see the mess the naughtiest
ever fairy had made.

POP!

All the townspeople
marched up to the well-behaved naughty fairy.

What a state! They were covered in slime and toffee and duckweed.

(The naughty fairy couldn't help but giggle).

"Are you responsible for this shambles?" demanded the Mayor.

"It's not my fault," complained the well-behaved naughty fairy. "I've been good, but my magic was naughty."

"Tidy this mess up," ordered Mrs Munchet.

"And no magic, or I'll turn you into a sausage!" added the naughty new friend.

Ignoring the naughty new friend, the well-behaved naughty fairy waved her magic wand to start the big tidy up, but...